To Maryanne, Stan, and Joni,
thank you for the pugs

To Noelle, Nick, Megan, and Blair,
thank you for the cat

And to Alex, Hana, and Marnie,
thank you for everything

—NVC

little bee books
an imprint of Bonnier Publishing USA

251 Park Avenue South, New York, NY 10010 | Copyright © 2018 by Nina Victor Crittenden
All rights reserved, including the right of reproduction in whole or in part in any form.
Little Bee Books is a trademark of Bonnier Publishing USA, and associated colophon is a trademark of Bonnier Publishing USA.
Manufactured in China   HH 1117 | First Edition
1 3 5 7 9 10 8 6 4 2
ISBN 978-1-4998-0529-1

Library of Congress Cataloging-in-Publication Data
Names: Crittenden, Nina Victor, author, illustrator. | Title: The three little pugs / by Nina Victor Crittenden. | Description: First edition. | New York,
NY: Little Bee Books, 2018. | Summary: Gordy, Jilly, and Zoie want to take their morning nap but a cat has taken over their basket. | Identifiers: LCCN
2017004956 | Subjects: | CYAC: Pug—Fiction. | Animals—Infancy—Fiction. | Cats—Fiction. | Naps (Sleep)—Fiction. | BISAC: JUVENILE FICTION / Animals
/ Dogs. | JUVENILE FICTION / Animals / Cats. | JUVENILE FICTION / Imagination & Play. | Classification: LCC PZ7.1.C745 Thr 2018 | DDC [E]—dc23
LC record available at https://lccn.loc.gov/2017004956

littlebeebooks.com
bonnierpublishingusa.com

# THE THREE Little Pugs

Nina Victor Crittenden

little bee books

Once upon a rug,
there were three little pugs.

Gordy loved to race,

Jilly loved to chase,

and Zoie loved to play
pug-o-war.

But they loved snoozing in their big,
cozy basket most of all.

When the three little pugs toddled over for their morning nap, they found the big bad cat in their basket! He stared at them with his big bad eyes.

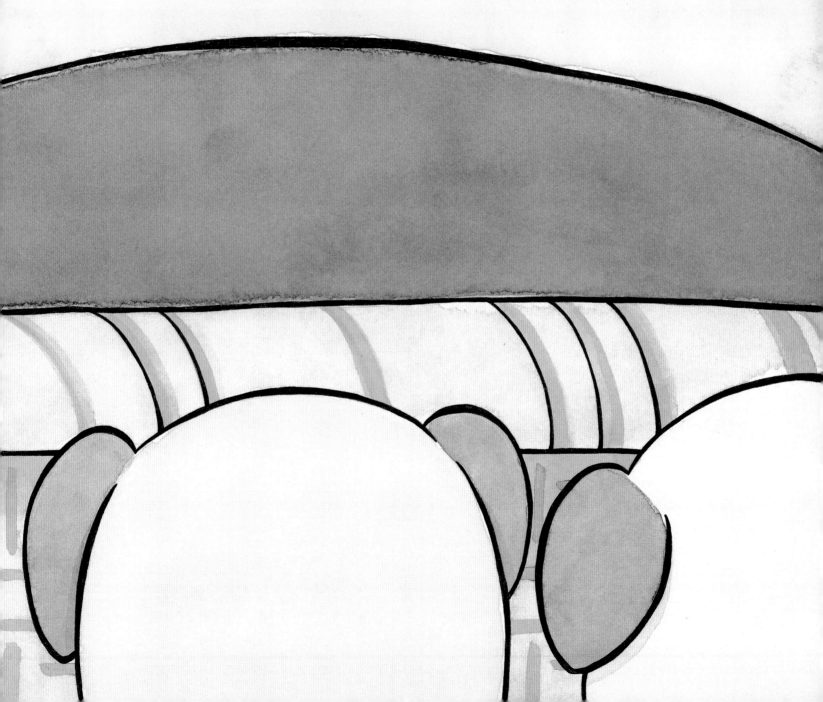

The three little pugs grumbled
under the love seat.

Luckily, Gordy had a sneaky plan
to get rid of the cat.

Three little tails wiggled.

When the big bad cat
drank some water . . .

. . . Gordy hurried and scurried and filled up
the basket with stripy straws, curly straws,
bendy straws, and swirly straws.

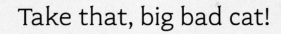

Take that, big bad cat!

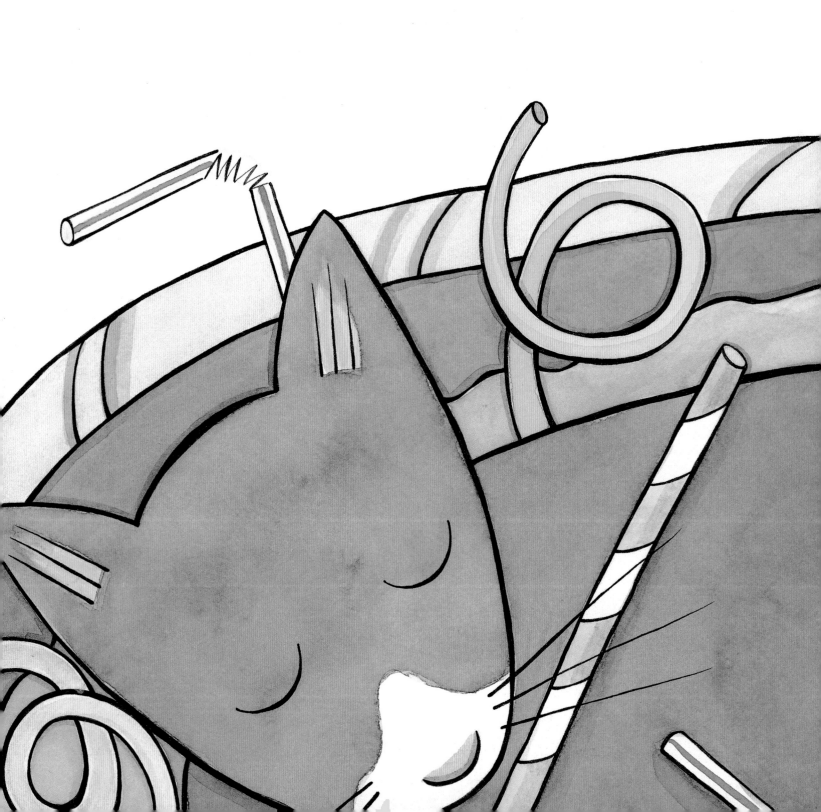

But the cat cuddled and snuggled
right into the basket.

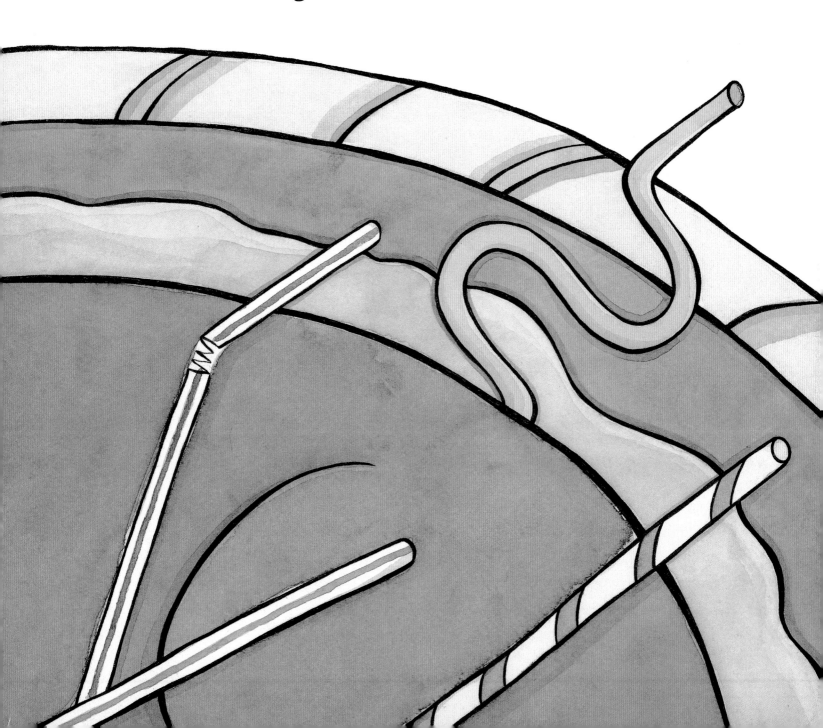

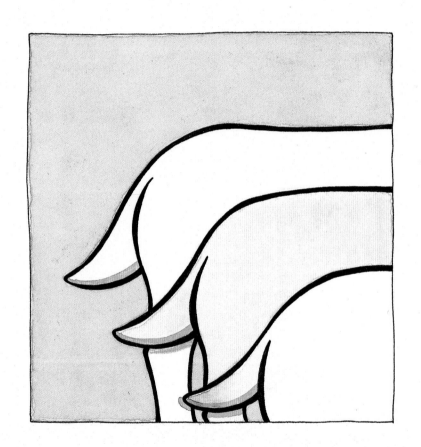

Three little tails drooped.

The three little pugs were really getting sleepy.

Luckily, Jilly had a sneaky plan
to get rid of the cat.

When the big
bad cat crunched
some kibble . . .

. . . Jilly hurried and scurried and filled up the basket with heavy sticks, light sticks, pointy sticks, and bright sticks.

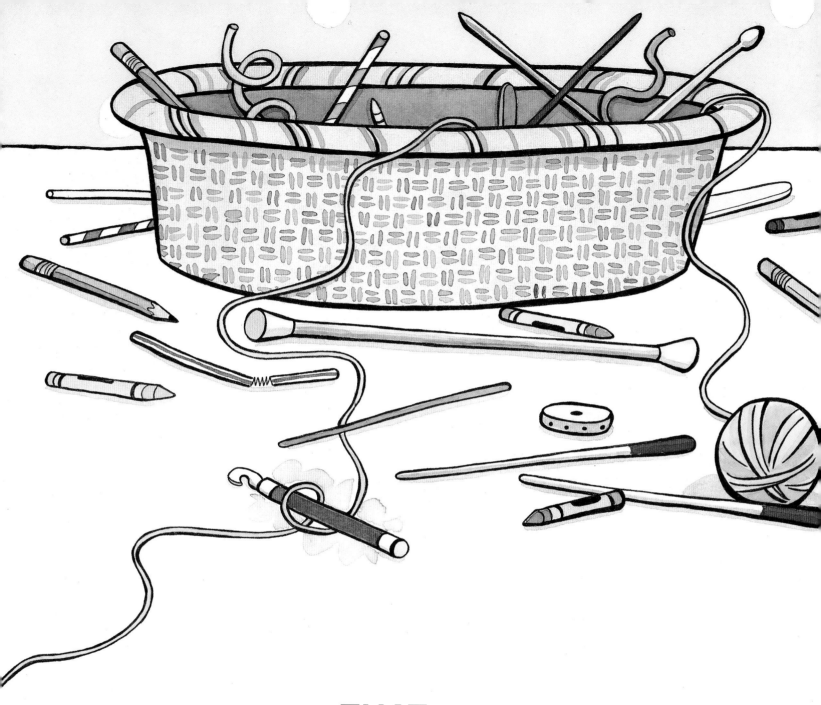

Take THAT, big bad cat!

But the cat cuddled and snuggled
right into the basket.

Three little tails lost their curls.

Now they had missed their
midmorning nap, too.

Luckily, Zoie had a sneaky
plan to get rid of the cat.

When the big bad cat watched the birdies . . .

. . . Zoie hurried and scurried and filled up
the basket with smooth bricks, lumpy bricks,
loose bricks, and clumpy bricks.

Take **THAT**, big bad cat!

But the cat cuddled and snuggled
right into the basket!

This was the **very last straw!**

Gordy, Jilly, and Zoie curled up their tails,
leaped off the love seat, and landed
right on top of the big bad cat.

And that was that.

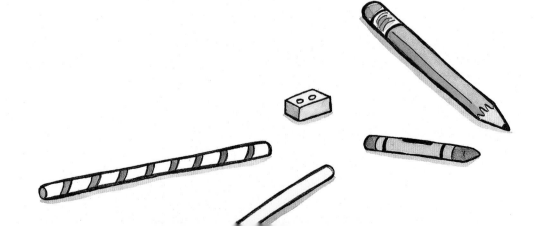

31901062711157